W9-BQZ-202

Peg

Other titles in the bunch:

Big Dog and Little Dog Go Sailing
Big Dog and Little Dog Visit the Moon
Colin and the Curly Claw
Dexter's Journey
Follow the Swallow
"Here I Am!" said Smedley

Horrible Haircut
Magic Lemonade
The Magnificent Mummies
Midnight in Memphis
Peg
Shoot!

Crabtree Publishing Company
www.crabtreebooks.com

PMB 16A, 350 Fifth Avenue
Suite 3308
New York, NY 10118

612 Welland Avenue
St. Catharines, Ontario
Canada, L2M 5V6

Stewart, Maddie.
    Peg / Maddie Stewart ; illustrated by Bee Willey.
        p. cm. -- (Blue Bananas)
        Summary: Peg the hen, who has only one leg, becomes an
unusual but much loved mother.
        ISBN 0-7787-0841-1 -- ISBN 0-7787-0887-X (pbk.)
        [1. Chickens--Fiction. 2. Mothers--Fiction. 3. Birds--Fiction. 4.
Physically handicapped--Fiction. 5. Stories in rhyme.] I. Willey,
Bee, ill. II. Title. III. Series.
PZ8.3.S854. Pe 2002
[E]--dc21
                                          2001032440
                                          LC

Published by Crabtree Publishing in 2002
First published in 1999 by Mammoth
an imprint of Egmont Children's Books Limited
Text copyright © Maddie Stewart 1999
Illustrations © Bee Willey 1999
The Author and Illustrator have asserted their moral rights.
Paperback ISBN 0-7787-0887-X
Reinforced Hardcover Binding ISBN 0-7787-0841-1

1 2 3 4 5 6 7 8 9 0 Printed in Italy 0 9 8 7 6 5 4 3 2 1

Peg.

Maddie Stewart

Illustrated by Bee Willey

Blue Bananas

For
the three boys on the farm,
Hal, Max and James.

M.S.

For Leopold.
Lots of love and XXX.

B.W.

Farmer Henry had hundreds of hens.

He didn't want Peg

She had only one leg.

So he left her behind

For the fox to find.

Benjamin Bottomly found her instead.

He carried her home

To a little warm bed.

What will I eat now?

7

Benjamin tucked Peg under his arm,

And took her to see his father's farm.

Pig fed her piglets.

Horse played with her foal.

The cat and her kittens

Licked milk from a bowl.

The cow and her calf were taking a stroll.

Peg felt sad that she wasn't a mother,

With chicks all around

To need her and love her.

Benjamin gently put Peg on the ground.

She hopped

And she flopped

oops

And she fell all around.

"What use am I?"

She began to cry.

"All floppy and wobbly

With only one leg."

And the others felt sorry

For poor little Peg.

Benjamin Bottomly said, "Don't cry!

Soon you'll be singing a sweet lullaby.

You shall have a family, dear little Peg,

For you don't need a leg to sit on an egg."

So Benjamin Bottomly

Asked here and there:

"Does anyone have any eggs to spare?"

"Here's one large egg

It came from the zoo,

But does that hen

Know what to do?"

"Know what to do?

Of course I do!

I'll sit on this egg

That comes from the zoo.

I'll keep it warm,

From dusk until dawn,

And when at last

My chick is born,

I'll give it my love

And I'll feed it my corn."

The chick that hatched grew big and fat.

He looked very cute in Benjamin's hat!

He loved his mother best of all.

He thought it was nice that she was small.

Benjamin Bottomly asked here and there:

"Does anyone have any eggs to spare?"

"I'll give you two,

All shiny and new.

But does that hen

Know what to do?"

Carry them carefully.

"Know what to do?

Of course I do!

I'll sit on these eggs

All shiny and new.

26

I'll keep them warm,

From dusk until dawn,

And when at last

My chicks are born,

I'll give them my love

And I'll feed them my corn."

Two little chicks

Hatched out soon.

On a sunny day

In the month of June.

As they got bigger

Their feathers grew

In brilliant colors

Of gold, green, and blue.

They spread their tails in the morning sun

As they preened and pranced

For their loving mom.

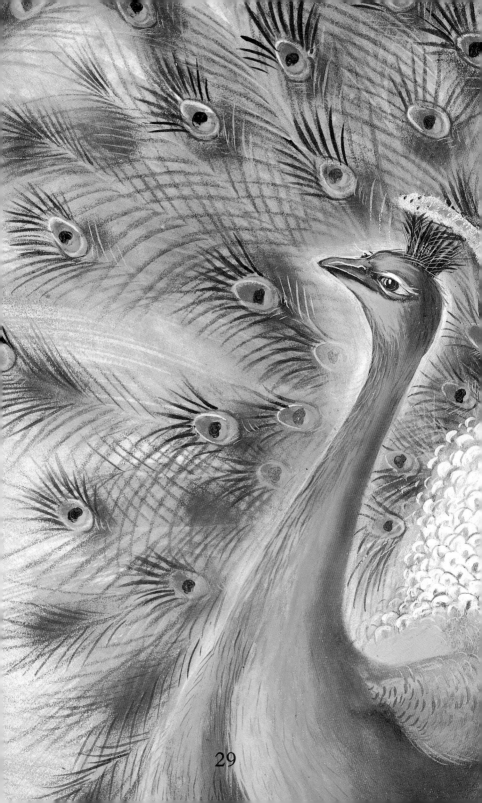

29

Benjamin Bottomly asked here and there:

"Does anyone else have eggs to spare?"

"I have a few, all speckled and blue.

But does that hen know what to do?"

soon Peg will have the biggest family on the farm.

"Know what to do?

Of course I do!

I'll sit on these eggs

All speckled and blue.

I'll keep them warm,

From dusk until dawn,

And when at last

My chicks are born,

I'll give them my love

And I'll feed them

My corn."

Three eggs cracked

And chicks were hatched.

The chicks grew bigger everyday

And chose the pond as a place to play.

They followed their mom
When she went for a toddle.

They thought her hop

Was a stylish waddle.

Still Benjamin Bottomly

Asked here and there:

"Does anyone have any eggs to spare?"

"I have four, I found on the floor.

But are you sure

You still want more?"

"Yes! I'm sure I still want more.

I want to mother chicks galore.

I'll sit on these eggs

You found on the floor.

I know how to do it,   One,

I've done it before!

I'll keep them warm,

From dusk until dawn,

And when at last my chicks are born,

I'll give them my love

And I'll feed them my corn." Two,

The eggs were hatched -

Three,

Four!

39

The chicks grew fast and learned to fly,

Up and away in the clear blue sky.

What a wonderful family you have, Peg

And as their mother hopped along,

They sang for her their sweetest song.

A beautiful hen,

All shiny and sleek,

Came into the farmyard

To take a peek.

Oh, no!
look who's
coming.

"And who is that hen

So floppy and lame,

So utterly useless

And horribly plain?"

That's our Mother

And we love her!